Heartlands

Chris Mann

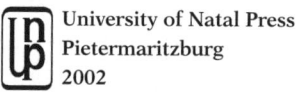

University of Natal Press
Pietermaritzburg
2002

Other work by Chris Mann

Poetry: *First Poems, New Shades, Kites, Mann Alive!, South Africans, The Horn of Plenty, The Roman Centurion's Good Friday.*

Plays in Verse: *The Sand Labyrinth, Mahoon's Testimony, Frail Care.*

Published by University of Natal Press
Private Bag X01, Scottsville 3209
South Africa
books@nu.ac.za
www.unpress.co.za

ISBN 1-86914-010-9

Cover design by Sumayya Essack, Dizzy Blue Dezign

Layout by Manoj Sookai

Printed and bound by Natal Witness Commercial Printers (Pty) Ltd, Pietermaritzburg

Contents

Acknowledgements

Versions of some of these poems appeared in the following publications whose editors are duly thanked: *Carapace, English Academy Review, Fidelities, New Coin, New Contrast, Rhodos* and the *Sunday Independent*.

The author would also like to thank the following for their help in the preparation of this volume: Alan Brimer, the late Guy Butler, Colin Gardner, Lynette Patterson, Jackie Shipster, Julia Skeen, Stephen Watson and Laurence Wright.

Further thanks are also due to the Arts and Culture Trust for a grant towards the costs of production.

ARTS &
CULTURE
TRUST

Duduma Pier

Midnight. A desolate pier.

The rust-pitted railing cold under the hand,
the ocean black and glassy,
widening out, out to the brim of the world.

The sky a great dishevelled emptiness,
the stars burning in loose white veils,
that strict edge of darkness along the horizon.

And riding in slowly, the swells,
long, silent, humped like dunes,
pulsing onwards in steady procession,
in a rhythm persistent as the turn of the seasons,
the roll of the earth and the moon's pale rise.

And then the dark rearing, a shudder, a wave-smash,
a sudden oceaning out of the stars,
white spray, black water flying,
suds glimmering fast over barnacled concrete,
the light of the navigation beacon obliterated
in a squall of tumultuous, battering noise.

Then slow through the dune-bush,
the walk back homewards,
that clench of the stomach when the sea crushed past,
that panic easing with the rhythm of the walking,
the rise of the moon and the sea's grey gleam.

And exuberance flowing in –
having bathed in the energy of the planet,
having trembled at the pulse-beat of a heart.

Midlands Lexicon

A winter's evening near the Kammasberg.
The crags duiker-grey. The air cut lemons.

You're out running. Tiny in the foot-hills.
Leaping over gullies. Splashing through grass.

You chant its names. Their open sesames,
their portals: *ingongon'; steekgras; aristida.*

Striding, sweating, you cross a quarry's ruins.
Angered by its strip-mine. The stews of trash.

A man with car-tyre sandals, hunting dogs
and rifle greets you on a path. Asks for *i-job.*

You start to dawdle. Relishing the views.
And breast a hill. Its grassed ascent to clouds.

Beside a gate – firewood bundles. Wattles.
Women with pangas and towel head-rings.

They talk *impilo* – 'health'. *Imvula* – 'rain'.
Their word-world explodes. In and around you.

You run deeper. Squelching a stream-bed's mud.
Glimpse, in a donga, a lourie's red wing-flash.

Then trotting past cattle, hear yourself grunt,
God, how I love, and fear, and owe this place.

You turn for home, loosened. Wording along.
Worded upon. Alive with lexicons. Their gates.

Their view-sites and quarries. Thickets and tools.
Their weapons. Head-rings. Lilies in mud. Wings.

Khamanga Metaphors

What mattered most
at Khamanga

wasn't just the dune-bush,
the sightings
through branches of sea;

the air-plants, the duiker
a hoof raised,
breathing dusk in a kloof.

What mattered most

wasn't even the throb-songs
of nightjars, calling
bird to bird in the dark,

or the quiet, the glimmering
above the estuary
of dim recessional stars.

What mattered most

was a firefly
pulsing in the bush-banks
its pinhead of life.

Dwebeza Hills

for John Gardener

You'd never think to find Dwebeza on a map.

That doesn't go to say Dwebeza isn't there,
for even if you never ford its drift
and bump across the cattle-grid into its hills,
you'll know the place I mean.

The aloe burning on a slope of lichened shale,
a warthog grubbing roots from dust,
the pair of eagles mating high above its thorns
will be as much as you'd expect.

But then strange scents, strange insects, plants and birds
will loosen your matrix of thoughts
until you start to hear, beyond the rocks and heat
the singing of the bush.

And when that night you lie down on the ground
beneath its huge, dark void of sky,
you'll shiver with a long-forgotten awe to see
its mass of glimmering stars.

This is the place which makes its presence felt
when labouring at a city desk
you yearn to wrench your tightened mind away
from files and grey-lit screens.

This is the place whose presence makes you say,
I want to drive across a drift
and walk through afternoons of singing bush,
and sleep beneath an open sky

and wake once more beneath Dwebeza's stars.

The Ruins of Mandulwana

You'll glimpse them in the space you grant to them,
a knee-high rubble of worked stones
across a hill-top on the plateau where you live.

Pied goats will watch you as you climb,
staring with cautious indifference
from the shade of boulders and flat-topped trees.

Reaching the walls, you'll turn and see
across the scrub and cattle on the plain below
a silent line of pale brown dust
which slowly lifts along the long straight road
between you and the nearest town.

It's then you'll slip off your backpack
and seated in the ghost-yard of a vanished home
will notice a small stone relic
among the ants and dassie droppings at your feet.
It will be warm and brown
and enigmatic with the centuries.

You'll feel vaguely dispirited,
wanting more from Africa's past,
wanting not to accept
how people feasting round a fire at night
their gourds and golden amulets
the smell of beer and roasting meat
the dancers laughing as they dance
are brought to such lonely oblivion
among such small and silent heaps of stone.

Africa and Europe do this, you think,
they keep on finding each other out.

You'll feel put in your place
and wander off from your companions
and want to get down on your knees
among the thorn-trees and the grass and stones.

The Magic of Motse

Motse for you was always just the pits.

A taxi-rank hell-hole, way out in a backveld,
with pitted streets, boarded-up shoe-shops,
the hawkers selling chicken heads and claws
and pigs browsing the seepage from drains.

Motse gave off a cloud, a stench of stories:
the mayor, his buses and the poverty fund,
the striking nurses and the school-bus crash,
the gang-rape of a girl by drunks with disease.

The shuttered bank, scrawled with slogans,
the public works office, its truck on bricks,
the magistrate's court and its tattered flag
were like the forts of a distant, troubled regime.

No wonder you'd always rush through Motse,
dreading the gunman in front of your bonnet,
hating the prejudice, the impatience it stirred
with fears of ancestral complicity, and blame.

But then you met someone who lives in Motse,
a short broad man, with a clean shaven head,
big eyes, big face, a laugh like a cloud-burst,
his neck all encrusted, like Job's, with boils.

This was Lesego, a teacher and catechist,
the founder of the burial and football clubs,
the maker of workshops for mothers and kids,
the new police forum, the literacy campaign.

So when, sometimes, you hear of Motse,
you can't help recalling its stories and drains.
But then you'll remember Lesego's committees,
his weekend workshops, his humour, his hope,

and Motse will change, change in front of your eyes.

Nanaggapoort Junction

You'd place its row of pepper-trees along a fence,
its platform, signal-box and waiting-rooms
some distance from the cities on a plain.

You stand there in a dream,
watching train after train slide in along the tracks
unload its passengers, then return.

Tika-tik, the carriages go, *tika-tik tika-tik.*

The passengers are thin and stooped
and wear no shoes
and shuffle past in silent crowds
and slowly board a line of rusted cattle trucks.

A tiny coughing skeleton of a boy,
with staring eyes and bulbous joints,
puts a small moist hand in yours and whispers,
'Remember us, the sick and dying.'

You rush off in a panic down the subway stairs,
so slowly, so slowly,
and find the station-officials and cry,
'But who are these people? Where are they bound?'

They study their clipboards a while,
then reply, 'What people? Which train?'

A diesel engine gives a banshee screech.
The trucks shudder, clunking dully,
then start to slide past, faster and faster
until dwindling down the narrowing tracks
they vanish in a pale oblivion of sky.

You waken, sweating, in your bed
and hear far off a train pass in the night.

Tika-tik, it goes, *tika-tik, tika-tik. Tika-tik, tika-tik.*

The Soega Road

You're bound to come across a Soega on your travels,
a sign beside a place that links your north and south,
a turn-off to a land of grass,
dry soils and succulents
that curls its rutted track between thick clumps of trees,
and flying down the fenced-in highway tar you'll say,
'I must make time to take the Soega Road one day.'

However much you think you know its whereabouts,
the Soega Road I'm getting at will take you unawares,
and while you're making up your mind
whether to brake and turn,
the farm-dam in the scrub, the dip-tank and the gums
will dwindle in the rear-view mirror of the car
and leave you trying to see a Soega where you are.

It's then the longing for its sprawl of hills revives,
the dance above its reeds of dragon-flies in spring,
the murmur in mimosa bush
of bees in flowering heat,
the acrid scent of herbs that hint the shades are near.
Who hasn't wished to drowse beneath a wild fig tree
and watch the weavers build and let their troubles be?

And then a different Soega starts to come in view,
the hills eroded wrecks that bone-bag cattle scour,
the watercourses choked with silt
and phosphates from the fields,
the co-op boarded up, the nurse and priest transferred,
the school-kids dressed in tatters, begging by the shop,
the district council offices a roofless, fire-charred shell.

But then still more of Soega will make its presence felt,
the farms and village firm with work for every home,
the people courteous on its paths
with time to talk and listen,
the doors of house and barn unlocked by day and night,
the ant-heap barren hills turned into mounds of grass,
the land a feast of mealies, pumpkins, meat and maas.

And when beside your road its sign takes shape again
and speeds in mist or noonday glare towards your car
you'll be time out of mind
still curious to take its turn,
and motoring on among the trucks, the cars and vans
that switchback home towards the city's rush and din,
you'll start once more to seek the Soega Road within.

The Mud Flats and Tides of Suurhoek

Low tide, the river shrunk to trickles, ebbing through reeds
and islets like rafts of purplish sedge in a flatland of mud
sweating out reeks in mid-summer heat of mud-rot and brine.

What a barefoot child, with a tin and a rod and a day to explore
imprinted were crabs sidling out the reeds with armoured claws,
barbed-wire snarls and rubble by a bank, and mud-prawn holes
dug in their thousands like machine-gun nests on a battle-ground.

What I absorb now, revisiting that shore, sends ripples back up
the rivers of Africa and hope again surging its tide of salt-water
and mullet and sheen across the mud-flats that sweat in my mind.

Komga Thornbush

More than the bellied white she-goat,
stretching her hunger into its thorns,
which flees as you climb out the car.

More than its silence, green in the heat.
The axe-scars down its bole.
The slow brown incendiaries of its pods.

More than the darkening chameleon
plodding its soft-pouched morsel,
its stegosaurus neck-ruff along a branch.

More than its wording, its saying:
umunga, soetdoring, hanyane,
mimosa, acacia karroo.

More than even its seepages
of amber and honey.
Its burning in a desert.

The plainchant of its bees.

Phosphorescence in Table Bay

Night sky like a cavity. Moonless. Dark as coal.
Car-lights down a hill. Street-lights on a beach.
Stars in a haze of white, down to the far horizon.

The bay was a mire, a quicksand of perils.
Tunny boats to port, reefs off to starboard.
A freighter like a silo, huge off the water.

My watch had ended. I sat on deck, feeling
the swell runs lifting and dropping the ship.
Watching distances, I murmured. Thinking

separates but love's the white green fire
seething the ocean. Love quickens. Joins.
I touched the sea-dew on the anchor cable

Boknes Chicory Oven

An undulance of hills. A glimpse of the sea.
Dune-bush in clumps, milkwood, *umunga*
reclaiming a stoep, a chimney's stump,
a room-sized oven's slow ruin of bricks.

Then in a redolence, a childhood memory
of roots being dried, the farmers emerge,
talking in a circle of hats and shorts,
foreboding nipping the heels of thoughts.

Hlambeza Pool

The pool is as you'd suppose it to be:
green and narrow, mirroring cycads
and ferns, the crags of a deep ravine.
Spined succulents thicket the banks,
the pleated rocks and surface shales.

And we are as you would imagine us,
sprawled on rugs with thermos flasks,
discussing new software and hardware,
exchanging stories of burn-out, stress,
armed robbery and patients with Aids.

'A green cathedral!' someone exclaims,
smacking at horseflies and mosquitoes.
The children pick through the rushes,
then clambering onto adult shoulders
leap out shrieking and splash the pool.

'What's *this*?' Bobbing along an edge,
roofed in by naves of ferns and reeds,
three fist-sized crumplings of paper,
pumpkin seeds in the boat of the one,
white beads and tobacco in the others.

'Offerings,' says a friend, 'you know,
like Greeks and Romans used to make.
Not to gods, to the people of the river,
the ancestors which Xhosa locals claim
are intercessors, their links with God.'

'Perhaps we shouldn't have swum here.'
The words reverberate across a silence.
I feel the cycad fronding of the unknown
breaking out around and inside us again,
then glimpse deep in a pool of memory

the faces of the living-dead, the shades.

The Clay Pits of Grahamstown

Crunching through scrub on the edge of town,
you'll curse the cavities gouged into the hills.
The vague whish of traffic from a bypass bridge
ebbs and flows in the air. Loose billows of smoke
spill out from the brick-fields towards the coast.

The pit at your feet is puddled like a strip-mine.
Its sides are squat cliffs, topped with mimosas.
You kick at a tin, the cartons and plastic bags
that garnish the roadside, duck through a fence
and trudge down a spiral ramp onto its terraces.

Its maw feels as lonely as a factory on Sunday.
Smears of oil around a tractor's dinged sump,
the head gear where yellow pay-loaders growl
to gulp their fill, the windows of the site-office
are powdered with ghostly vestiges of its talc.

The kaolin's the white of plaster of Paris.
Dissolved in rain-water, between the ridges
and chevrons of truck and tractor spoors,
it has the dulled glint of a kitchen's sullage.
Fingered, it feels viscous and silky as saliva.

Trucks of it, sewn up and stacked in sacks,
rumble past the hedges of the town at night,
to cities whose culture has the land in it grip,
that cannot leave off: the clay-pit's built into
the keyboard I tap, the page, the ink you read.

Sterkfontein Ancestor

There's little splendour in the sight of splintered bones
chipped stick-like from the oozing limestone of a cave.
There's less to hear that where you lie was once a kloof
and shoved or slipping from its heights, you died alone.

Aeons before our blood-line forged its hoes and spears,
you'd loped between the ferns and antheaps of the plain,
and even if they prise a mustier cranium from earthed time
you're now the oldest human wraith to crack its fossil beds.

Trembling at night up trees, to smell warm fur upwind,
could you foresee the offspring of your huddled troop
would populate and rule the earth, and walk the moon?
Did you kill kin like fleas, and groan like us for peace?

I grunt to think our hands, our spines and bulbous brains
unfolded from the genes of you, with words and dreams,
the aching backs that still aren't used to standing straight,
the gloomy moods at dusk which make us grab a drink.

Did you fear death and teach your young? I bet you did.
Was life less frantic then? We've heard that it was short.
We like to think that we've improved and that our brows
and drives aren't quite a low as yours. I stretch a hand

across three million years and touch your ruin and hear
the flesh-beasts howl and see you back into the thorns,
pressing a child's soft skull into your long-haired breasts.
You sweat with fear, aggression, a furious will to survive,

you – our Earth Madonna, and shade released from stone.

The Dunes of Woody Cape

The dunes spread out their hills before you as you look at them.
Slope after scalloped slope of sand, further than the eye can see.

From where you climb, the view takes in the sea and its horizon.
Slowly, the molten wrinkling of the swells crumples on the shore.

You scoop up a handful of the hot sand, and run it into a palm.
The granules are the brown, the white and orange of sea-shells.

Faint memories of geological time-spans drift in, but do not fix.
You lift your head. The furthest dunes are white as a cuttle-fish.

The nearest are fawn, bleached fawn. They shoulder above you.
Sprouts of sea-grass and light green, spiky reeds adorn their base.

You could be on an outing, in a garden of meditation writ large.
Its boulders are clumps of milkwood, its raked floor is the sand.

Calm rinses steadily through you. What follows could be grace.
And then you're ready, to turn and go back into the hurly-burly.

Bees in the Wheatlands of Genadendal

Facts are things you read in books and find on screens.
They're what the well-schooled mind turns nature into,
the cells of a wing, the proteins and minerals of wheat.

But truths are much livelier, much touchier than facts.
Truths are the bees that brood in the heart's deep hive
and fly the beebread and honey of their foraging there.

Some hold that facts are the hard and software of science.
Stick to the facts they say, for truth is so very subjective.
I say: show me the field or thought not pollinated by bees.

Heraclitan Heresies

1

So what if map and satellite
can fix your place in space and time?

For you and all you know are flux,
with water, fire and earth and air.

Listen: can you not hear the surf
grinding the coast of Greece to dust?

Watch: can you not see India's drift
slowly ramming Tibet into the sky?

2

Lead me to the moral high ground
and I will climb the rainbow's arch.

Isolate the causes of war
and I'll nail down the shifting sea.

3

Is life not flux sinewed by strife?
Is strife not bonded in the One,

as stress binds opposites by day,
and sciamachy riddles night?

Save your breath. The abstract-minded
have made a God of Plato's forms

and cannot hear you on your beach
shouting Homer into a gale.

Pholela Field

It brings you its cattle
bunched at a salt-lick
dipping their heads
on a slope of kikuyu,
and odours of dung,
ammonia and silage
layered into the scent
of honey from hives
in the gum plantation on a hill.

It shows you its weeds
sinewy and restorative
in a shed's brick floor,
worm-cast pit-heads,
a mulch of old grass
rotting into new tilth
and clans of midges
dancing in courtship
above the husks of their past.

It induces memories,
of digging cartridges,
the brass still acrid,
from bushed-in forts,
of ancestors in caps,
galoshes and aprons
swilling out cow-stalls
with wooden buckets
in Irish and Devonshire mists.

It brings you sunlight
at a journey's end
feeding its leaf-life.
It offers you its air
and the impalpable
free grip of gravity
holding together
the soil and river,
the earth and the sky and you.

Hogsback Oracle

in memoriam Monica Wilson

Who can discern their clan,
its shibboleths and ghosts,
until they encounter another?

Hers was a pastoral people.
Living with them in youth
she looked, asked and wrote.

How did they value land?
Their children? Each other?
What had conquest done?

Trim, fastidious and spry
she had a scholar's gravitas,
the spirited gaze of a nun.

Her Rome was Cambridge.
Widowed long she made
the Hogsback her Zion.

Her findings were her life:
small-scale clans to flourish
need to unfold in the large.

*

Seymour

in memoriam Donald White

1

Too small to be a dorp, too dry
and Eastern Cape for a village,
its outline trembles on hot days.

In Xhosa it's known as *Mpofu*,
which hints at dun, austere colours,
the eland's name, and nourishment.

Its dam, its row of scraggy gums
and corrugated-iron rooftops
are perched below escarpment crags.

The view, across aloed thorn-veld
down to the coastal-plain goes on
and on until you see cloud shadow

scudding slowly towards the sea,
until the land and sky are hazed
and sight and vision start to blur.

2

The orchards of the orange farm
that you, your father and brother
built with the farmhands in the bush

greened the riverine soils below.
Once, over a beer, you told me
that years ago, before the change,

your farmer friends and families
would motor up the mountain pass
and weekend at the small hotel,

piling a bakkie with youngsters,
gillies, fishing tackle and meat.
'Hell,' you said, 'but what a party!'

3

One searing afternoon last March,
I slowed and took the Seymour turn,
wanting a break, a drink, a phone.

Its single street was much the same,
a scratch on shale where little stirred
except, this time, for listless goats

chewing a shrub in someone's yard,
plastic bags spiked on thorn-bushes
and stock that grazed a rubbish dump.

I parked and walked across the dust.
The co-op's door had been torn off,
its rows of window panes smashed in.

The public phone hissed on its hook.
A drunk snored in the empty bar,
face down among a slew of quarts.

The radio in the hotel foyer
was gabbling on about football
being played before a Joburg crowd.

The manager appeared in socks,
declined my bid to purchase tea
yawned and scratched a shirtless chest.

4

It was the nightmare of your caste,
the post-uhuru slide from hopes
of jobs, clinics, houses and cars

to run-down courts and hospitals,
armed thieves and dark imaginings
of plague, looting and malls on fire.

As I reversed and bumped away
you with your grey-blue eyes Donald
returned to haunt me with a laugh.

'So? Didn't I warn you?' you asked.
And I, that frayed riposte, 'Was there
a choice? Besides, we're different

and hands long bound are always limp.'
The sun ovened the mountain air,
the road seemed steeper than before.

Prickling with sweat, I drove slowly,
scheming like the hunter-gatherers,
the pastoralists who came before

ways to survive in that landscape,
to extricate vision from sight
and track the eland through the thorns.

Grahamstown Sage

to Guy Butler on his eightieth birthday

What man is this, who eight decades since birth,
his pulse-beat weak and fluttering through old age,
still treads with cautious zest his patch of earth
and does not deign to grieve his health – or rage?

Unsettled most by those who settle least
the Africa that droughts and feeds his soul,
he shakespeared students in his thorny east,
and linked the native writer to the metropole.

The institutes he built on Grahamstown's clay
were visioned first inside his poet's heart.
His creativity's a gullied sea whose spray
is pressed into the pages of his art.

Their theme's the secret of the joy he gives:
he loves the place and people where he lives.

Billboards and Crash, Johannesburg Airport

The wipers flick-flack, flick-flack their fan-shaped holes in the storm.
Ahead, four lanes of rush-hour traffic, slowing along the oil-dark tar.
You clutch and brake, change down, stretch over the steering-wheel
And wipe a ragged circle in the windscreen mist that blurs the scene.

And there they are, on either side the airport highway, the billboards.
Bolted onto girders, and towering above the off-ramps and factories,
Above the rapidly rotating flashes of blue and red you shish towards.
Creeping, braking, your gut tensing as you think of missing the plane.

The low torn speeding clouds of an evening sky silhouette the boards.
Their wide rectangular screens of images tower unshaken in the wind.
Their rows of floodlights, on the brackets below the company slogans,
Shine up into the rain, turning the drops into long thin silvery streaks.

The road's a mall of huge computers and cars, a titan eating burgers.
Beside a fly-over, a bare-chested athlete offers you his deodorant can.
Sheep with tags in their ear-lobes travel near you, staggering in trucks.
Above their shorn skin, the eyes of a billboard Venus gaze into yours.

Smiling above the traffic, she holds out a bank's plastic wafer of card.
You ease alongside ambulances and fire-trucks, a mess of crushed cars.
Look down and for one long ghastly moment see a man's pulped head.
His body's strapped onto a stretcher. Rain and blood mix on hi cheeks.

Where is he now, you wonder. At the party in the billboard above him?
The guests braai chops, lift beers. Seem happy, healthy, forever young.
You think of Plato's cave. Of ads in stained-glass windows. Drive on.
Past paramedics, in orange bibs, trying to tape a drip-feed into his arm.

Karroo Pyre

in memoriam Sipho Hashe,
Qaqawuli Godolozi and Champion Galela

This is the place where the Pebco Three were shot and burned.
Look, this patch of earth beside a farm road on an arid plateau.
Can you not see the ash of the thorn-wood pyre and their bodies?

How faint a grey-white memento of those who were so animate.
Their sepulchre is a barbed-wire fence, a bush and the open sky.
Their threnody's the wind and the whooping at night of a jackal.

Imagine the thick sprinkle of the stars on the night of their death
And police in jeans and running shoes with pistols in their belts
Heaving the warm limp bodies with heads dangling onto the fire.

Imagine the policemen taking chops and sausages out their vans,
Pulling the rings on cans of cold beer and talking sport and kids,
Braaing around their own thorn fire until the corpses were burnt.

Here is a beer-can of that night, thrown under a bush by the fence.
And blown against an aloe, one of the punnets that held the meat.
And look, sniffing across the scrub, here are the ghosts of the kudu.

Why are we who are so murderous so condescending about them?
They are beautiful in the elegance of their muzzles and their horns
And beautiful in that they joust but do not kill each other in droves.

Oh you who stop on this road and mourn for what happened here
Weep for the Pebco Three but do not weep for them or theirs alone.
Weep for the creature who unlike the kudu slays its kin in droves.

Carpark Oyster-Sellers

The man is tall and thin. He's limping from a cut on his foot.
The woman wears a doek. She looks too old to be pregnant.
The infant on her back has the orange halo of kwashiorkor.

They are working the carpark beside the Fish River mouth.
The woman scuttles across to your car. She holds up a bag.
A few small oysters are lying there on folds of damp hessian.

You want to be unprejudiced. To improve on your ancestors.
It's not going to be easy. Her lips are pale from sipping meths.
The oysters look like crabs, tiny grey crabs without any legs.

'Please, my bossie,' she says. 'Me and my family is hungry.'
You hate the blank-faced demeanour you use to distance her.
You wince at the obsequious charade she starts to perform.

The man coughs and spits on the ground. His stare is sullen.
His eyes are looking for yours. You catch the reek of liquor.
Would Millais have painted them, stripping the oyster-beds?

You spurn oysters. Their sea-weed taste, phlegm-like texture.
Hand-outs also. Training, job-creation – isn't that the answer?
You're scared to think that they are lepers and you a pharisee.

Behind their heads, blue sea, white sand stretching for miles.
They were out there before day-break, to catch the low-tide.
It would be mawkish to depict them bare-headed and praying.

You've heard their people work the Plata, the Ganges and Nile.
'Please, my bossie,' she says, 'my childrens is so very hungry.'
There's no evading them. Their infant wakes with a long wail.

Unveiling a KwaNamatha Shade

The scene registers: a hilltop plot of grass,
cleared and fenced, choirboys in cassocks,
a priest with glasses, then Thisha Ngcobo
standing at a tombstone veiled with a sheet.

That much the painting before me evokes.
A stippling of ink's the flint in the grave.
Pale floatings of colour, textures of light
become fawn grass, a blue KwaZulu sky.

It looks so real. Thorn-trees and rondavels,
the tense, sombre look on the teacher's face
cross over a then to now, a there to a here,
with traces of clouds and barbs on the wire.

The art is in the omissions. The goats I saw
straying into a neighbour's maize are gone.
So have the friends that crowded the fence,
a bus with balloons, thumping to a wedding.

Under the level flint, the coffined residue
of Ngcobo's father lies. The grieving over,
the money saved up to purchase the tomb,
he's being returned, back home as a shade.

Dogs barking nearby, the ads from radios,
the prayers and hymns have leached away.
He like the painting has now turned into
a clustering of hints, a presence of clues.

Wording the Gap in the Hinterlands

A landscape of aloes and thorns,
the stoep of the post office in town.

Two fellow teachers from the school,
having sat beside you on the bench,

are reading a gloss-faced postcard
sent by a friend studying abroad.

First they, in an English collage,
then you, in minimalist Xhosa

struggle to express a response
to water lilies, a bridge, a stream.

A pause, a silence like a kloof
suddenly chasms apart your talk.

You sense the borders of wordscapes,
of unpainted lands within a land.

Words – how they undo and make us,
as much the frontier as the pioneer.

Saying Goodbye to the Romans

1

The day the Romans left
they marched their standards to their ships.

Most people ran out of their doors and cheered.

Some hotheads painted their faces with woad,
looted the mead in a tavern
and hanged a few collaborators in the woods.

That was, I suppose, to be expected:
after hundreds of years of Roman oppression
it could have been worse, much worse.

It was so exhilarating – to be free!

No longer paying tax to foreigners,
powerless to stop the worst of their merchants
enticing young girls behind the haystacks
with figs from Syria, and wine from Gaul.

No longer fearful of their swaggering soldiers
killing off dissidents in their barracks
before the new proconsul did his rounds.

And no more cringing, in front of magistrates
who'd take such pleasure, such jovial pleasure
in asking how many of us could read or write
or build a level road before they came.

As if our worth as a people
could ever be judged by such things!

Good riddance to their arrogance I say.

Were we not happier, and more considerate
before the Romans came?

2

Now there is work – real work ahead,
cutting their tariffs on our wheat and tin,
placing our people in the new institutions,
curbing the inrush of bordering clans
and luring tutors, from Rome and Greece
to teach our youth their baffling tongues,
their tricks of governance, their money lore.

Panes of glass – in a turf-roofed hovel!

I go to bed exhilarated, but ill at ease.

How can we show dalesman and chief
that there is no going back to the tribe?

How can we persuade the wild young zealots
to stop harassing the Romans who've stayed
and help us build these things called towns?

3

And so, in a way, I have begun to miss them.

Despite the cold abstractions of their speech
and their insufferable belief, that to advance
we'd have to take Rome into our hearts,
I have, I suppose, begun to miss them.

But why? I hear the martyred rebels ask.

The people, scythes in hand at my door
that's why – glaring at me as they complain
of empty plates and unworked fields,
of posts restricted to certain bloodlines
and bribes extracted by petty officials.

As if an end to the Romans
could bring improvements to the soul!

Ha – even the druids. When they shake fists
at the loose behaviour in the settlements
and the mad expectation, burning the youth
that life should get better with every year
I miss, in a way, an old if bitter consolation.

I miss being able to shrug and say,
Not us, not us, the Romans are to blame.

First Memories of Place

They're archaeological sites,
sedimented in the mudflats
and cave-beds of personal time.

Like spoor sealed on a tidal bank,
a pot's clay lug, smothered in scree,
they wait the daylight of a dig.

To fossick in my sites retrieves
vague relics of the phantom shapes
which stalked my fern and cycad years.

I'd have been sitting up in bed
to silt away the first that firmed.
A sash window, roof-tops at dusk,

my parents clicking off the light
must all be there. All are missing.
The fossil's this: a pavement gum,

a streetlight winking in the leaves,
and jostling on the bunk-bed wall,
as in a cave, light-flecks, shadows.

Landing at Ithaca

You find it strange that I should still love words,
should eat as bread the poetry of books and speech
and mutter on for hours to metaphor fresh verse
when language to our kin means data, skill or tool.

Like them I stare into the whirlpools of lit screens
and raft into the strange new sights of cyber skies
where Lotus-shores of images enthral the mind
and souls like Ulysses' lie drugged upon a couch.

My soul, like his, still numbly feels a distant tug
towards a sea-born rugged isle, an Ithaca of words.
I struggle back, and landing find inside the hall
a nurse and wife, a parent, prophet and a child.

Their tears and questioning, their rancour and embrace
bring home where I have been, and who I have become.

To — in the Supermarket

Ah strange, distant and beautiful woman,
pushing a trolley down an avenue of tins,
a child in tow, a shopping list in hand,

how much I adore the curve of your waist,
the sway of your body, the pause, the turn
and reed-quick bending to one side of you.

Let me pile your trolley with new-baked rolls
and fill your arms with artichokes and wine.
Let me explain that thinking you elsewhere

but finding you here has torn the membrane
that custom and routine thickens in my eyes.
And through the fissure bursts, as at the first,

the whole breathing, talking, hurrying, laughing,
soft-lipped, warm-hipped, red-scarfed woman of you.

Child on a Swing in a Durban Suburb

Dank mist. Ghost lawn. Faint outlines of trees.
The sibilance of traffic from distant highways.
A fusillade of barking, fading down the hedge.

You for the first time were no more a nape,
a frailty of shoulders and a squeal of infancy
sent flying away from me and swooping back.

You'd trotted off into the mist on your own,
had climbed on the tyre and hands on ropes,
stood on the threshold of a door to the sky.

I came out on the stoep and stared in silence,
the parent delighting in the child's delight,
wanting to help you and terrified you'd fall.

I moved towards you, stopped and hesitated.
Were my knots safe? The grass was perilous
with gale-torn twigs and ship-wreck boughs.

I struggled like now to gauge right distance,
wanting you to grow, but not be damaged
as the green wastage of avocados in grass.

You saw me, waved, bent knees and shoved.
Your airship yawed, lurched and then took off.
I stood inside, watching you sing as you flew.

Homework in Frances Street

He's stooped above his roll-top desk,
writing, a bald man with glasses,
a clipped-back prickle of moustache.
I'm walking through a dim threshold,
a cup of coffee wisping in my hand.
He turns and smiles across the years,

Grandpa, back home, in his office.
Receipts and invoices are bulked
on spikes like hayricks on the desk.
Frizzes of wool from the warehouse,
stuck onto sample cards, are strewn
with files and car parts on the floor.

Tacked above the pigeon-hole store
of tools, gun-oil rags, dowsing twigs,
his hand-written sign: *Concentrate.*
I put the coffee down and glimpse
precise blue strokes and curls of ink
in columns down a ledger's page.

The memory ebbs in my thoughts
as spelling-book in hand I call
across my ten-year-old son's room.
Take-away wrappings trash a shelf.
Socks, shorts, Lego, a hard-disc drive,
its casing stripped, chaos the floor.

I watch his wild, erratic script
as feet hanging over the bunk
he toils towards tomorrow's test.
Then hear myself repeat to him
a mantra for my own deep scrawl:
Concentrate, I say, *Concentrate.*

Places

A place is what you make of it:
the shale beside that arid stream
where shaking out a folded rug
you and the passion facing you
began to talk of building trust
and smelt wild honey in the air
and lingered kissing in a kloof
of bitter aloes, rocks and thorns.

A place is what it makes of you:
that town of rusted factory gates
and drizzle drifting over shacks
where in the office late at night
you added up the year-end loss
and said, 'Enough, we can't go on,'
and put your head down on the desk
and felt an ulcer twist its knife.

Beyond such places wait the walls,
the doors and mirrors of a home,
where one morning in the passage,
still drowsy from a troubled sleep,
you turned on opening your door,
and saw, as if not there till then,
the knotted boards along the floor
and dust-motes burning in the sun.

Rini Bougainvilleas

Late spring, the bougainvilleas
in lank, thorn-spined clusters
of purple, crimson and orange
sprout in Grahamstown's streets.

The rains gone, a berg wind
gushes dry heat through town,
wilting bean-shoots and roses,
sealing the soil to baked clay.

This is the season of dread,
when frontier fears revive.
Touching the window-bars,
you wince at the shoot-outs

and rape on the midday news
and watch across the street
a slow shadow whose young
live overseas chain her gate.

What is indigenous endures,
you think, but what endures
becomes like bougainvillea
indigenous within its niche.

Beside the crust of a lawn
a cycad's armoured innards,
an ant-heap's domed vitals
tortoise through the hours.

A Field in Italy

1

I'm standing in a field in Italy.
A hot summer's day.
Crows. Tractors.
Poplars lining a river.
Clods and stubble at my feet.

The trees are as in his diary.
The gravel farm road.
The narrow canals.
The soft quick plop of frogs
arrowing into a ditch.

I'm standing near Venice
with people in a field.
The sky is cloudless,
as blue as Giotto's
frescoed inside a dome.

A painter's skies.
Spacious. Visionary.
Opening above the plains,
the mountains of a Europe
for once at peace.

I'm standing in a field in Italy
trying to grasp what's happening.
The heat off the soil
beats into my face as at home.
A taxi is parked in the trees.

Go to the gaps for the poem.
The words throb in my thoughts.
Like a mantra. A headache.
The hook of a song
I cannot quieten. Or end.

The people around me
are talking in blurs.
They look confused.
The snapshot they hold
no longer matches the field.

2

Their language whirls past me.
My thoughts unfold.
I've come from South Africa
with wife and children
as pilgrims to this field.

We're here to give thanks.
Thanks to a family
who sheltered my father
for two years of a war,
risking a bullet in the head.

I want our son and daughter
to meet their young.
To see the field he slept in.
The ruin that housed them.
The pigsty where he hid.

'Ma tanti anni fa, sai.'
Signora Ferro's beside me.
'The barn was here,' she says.
'Or maybe closer to the trees.
It's all so long ago.'

My Italian is rough and slow.
Her dialect's a rapid.
Our talk leads to guesses.
Confusion. Laughter.
Scraps of knowing. Then gaps.

3

I look across her shoulder
and see him. My father.
Hiding all night in the reeds.
His jacket's wet sacking,
his shirt a damp shroud.

He lies curled up on his side
and breathes in the cap
pulled over his face.
Only his breath is warm.
His will to survive is the fire.

There are soldiers with dogs
billeted in the farmhouse
a hundred steps from the reeds.
Informers on bicycles.
Manhunts at dawn.

He's slept in rain for a month.
A vagabond. A scavenger.
A soldier with a cause
chest-deep and sinking
in the dark abysmal bog of war.

He trusts no one.
He thinks like a spy on the run.
Where will I hide myself next?
What can I eat?
Who will betray me? When?

He thinks of his parents.
He yearns for his friends.
The young war-bride
waving waving on the pier
who is my mother.

She that night is also on guard.
Hunched in a bunker
above Port Elizabeth's bay.
Scanning the sea in a screen
for blips of submarines.

The army has written.
He's missing. Thought dead.
The handsome young soldier
to her a wound. A void.
Beneath a southern Orion.

I see her in her headphones
grieving, longing
each time I drive that road
and glimpse through dune-bush
that wan grey remnant of war.

He blows alive in his thoughts
small coals of hope
then hears across the field
the croak of sepulchral crows.
Despair seeps back like mist.

4

His diary's factual. Laconic.
I sense his moods in the gaps.
He hides its tracks of a self,
its spoor of an epoch
in holes he digs in the field.

He writes of food and rain.
Of prisoners found on a farm,
instructed to watch
the family who hid them
shot in front of their barn.

Haggard, fugitive prisoners.
South Africans like him
sent running in a field
a stubble of maize.
Shot in the back as they ran.

A family has offered him help.
Signora Ferro's.
Her grandfather's a foreman,
deep-eyed, unlettered.
Fear kwashiorkors their sleep.

They room in an outhouse,
with cattle, rats and birds.
They eat polenta and beans.
The pigs and they eat water
when there's no food.

My father wants their food,
their warning whispers.
They want him invisible.
He hides in haystacks. Reeds.
With pigs in a sty.

I look again in the reeds.
He's crouched on his heels,
squeezing his hands.
The cap's back on his head.
He looks so thin, so cold.

I've come to this field in Italy
in search of this presence.
This shade. My father's.
The soldier, cricketer, hero
who died when I was four.

The man in a wide lapel suit,
his hat at a jaunty angle,
a suitcase packed for hospital
waving in the doorway
at the end of the passage at home.

Smiling and waving waving
to me at infancy's end,
sitting with a wind-up truck,
toy soldiers and cattle
on a strip of brown linoleum.

Numbed by a child's intuition
that something unspeakable
was happening to the adults.
To us. To him. A felt absence.
A gap, among the rest.

5

The memory shallows. Fades.
I hear Signora Ferro talking,
far off, in swirls of words.
Stocky. Black-haired. Resolute.
A handbag over one arm.

The talking slows. Boils on.
I feel again at a distance,
apprehensive. Lost.
Bahlala beshiyana abantu,
I hear in my thoughts.

People keep leaving each other,
the words in Zulu put it.
Humans keep missing others.
Dangling raw ends.
Loneliness. Suspicion. Gaps.

40

We walk on into the field.
It twists our thin-soled shoes.
I look down at the clods
and think of the blood
anointing Europe's fields.

Ten million people dead,
the First World War. Or twelve.
Forty million, the Second.
Or is it sixty? Who knows.
Can stop to count, or care.

Numbers, numbers, I think.
Their calm precision. Their penury.
Impoverishing feelings.
Distancing air-raids, mine-fields.
Ghosting the horror. The dead.

Signora Ferro looks dismayed.
The trees and canals are there,
the gaunt padrone's house.
But outhouse, threshing yard,
pig-sties are gone. Are gaps.

6

I look away across the river.
Field after field of maize.
Head-high, tasselled and green.
Like rank on rank of soldiers
in oblongs and squares.

Like soldiers on the march.
Neanderthals. Etruscans.
Romans. Vandals. Huns.
Occupying the passes,
invading villages and plains.

They tramp on into the present.
Not far from the field
armies from Russia and America
are camped in Bosnian woods,
policing ferocious tribes.

I stumble over the clods.
The disc-plough's compressed
one side of their chunks.
It gleams dully. Like leather,
or bronze or toughened steel.

Like the helmets of soldiers
half-buried in the soil.
The clods' other side is irregular.
Like faces smashed off
in personal holocausts of lead.

I look up from my feet.
The clods are thick in the fields
that stretch across the plains
beyond the crinkle of the Alps,
to Auschwitz, the Somme.

Above them, amplitudes of sky.
Tranquillity like a reprimand.
A silent reproach.
To people at war, to armies
slaughtering under the dome.

7

I murmur to my wife:
'The earth's small canopy of air,
the vacuum dark beyond.'
'The sky is bluer,' she says
'than skies at home.'

The comment sticks,
unties a cluster of fears.
My thoughts again lurch
on gaps, on the rifts
between the people at home.

Their hungers, animosities,
smouldering prejudice.
The retrovirus of violence
clubbing a head to a pulp
in farmhouse, subway, shebeen.

The children tug at my arm.
'What's happening?' they ask.
I've read them the diary,
shown them the bunker,
the canal he swam at night.

They've played with their peers.
Football. Water-pistols.
The story's entered their lives.
But now they are restless.
Looking for openings. Fun.

8

Signora asks if we're ready
then takes me by the arm.
Gaps are loosening edges,
are closing. For now.
I shut my eyes and see him.

My father. Standing in the reeds.
Hands in armpits, waiting.
I sense he is with me, of me
much more than before.
I am ready. To see him home.

I open my eyes. To sunlight.
Trees. Families in a field.
Across the hot furrows
irrigation sprays are clattering,
lifting bright water in the air,

showering fresh sprigs of green.
The families turn.
We hug. Slowly. One by one.
Then walk in silence to the taxi
across the ploughed field.

Four Places One Colour

Dwesa

The beach.
Evening.

Tall waves
crashing on the shore.

And cast up on the sand
a scrap of porcelain

pounded
rounded

still blue.

Kap River

Suddenly poised
above the river's long rippling

a thumb-sized glitter

that drops

and

kills

in a thrash of silver and blue.

Embo

A curve of candle-flickered earthen wall.

Two men and a woman
a child
asleep on the back of a girl

their shadows
hovering as the ancestors behind them.

And heaped in a pale grey metal bowl
the bowels of a goat

moist, infolding

red and blue.

Steelpoort

Above a silhouette of mine-shafts

slime-dams
mine-dumps

corrugated-iron roofs
tall shaggy gums

an evening sky
like a loving rebuke

dissolving
embracing

rose-blue.